JOURNEY TO CRYSTAL MOUNTAIN

A MIDDLE GRADE LITRPG FANTASY ADVENTURE

THE CRYSTAL MOUNTAIN SAGA
BOOK 1

TIMOTHY MCGOWEN

ILLUSTRATED BY
CANDACE MORRIS

EDITED BY
CANDACE MORRIS

RISING TOWER BOOKS

Fantasy / LitRPG / Gamelit

BIBLIOGRAPHY OF TIMOTHY MCGOWEN

HAVEN CHRONICLES

Haven Chronicles: Eldritch Knight

SHORT STORIES/NOVELLAS

Dead Man's Bounty

THE CRYSTAL MOUNTAIN SAGA

Journey To Crystal Mountain Book 1

LAST BORN OF KI'DARTH

Reincarnation: A Litrpg/Gamelit Trilogy
Rebellion: A Litrpg/Gamelit Trilogy
Retribution: A Litrpg/Gamelit Trilogy

ORDER & CHAOS

Arcane Knight Book 1: An Epic LITRPG Fantasy
Arcane Knight Book 2: An Epic LITRPG Fantasy
Arcane Knight Book 3: An Epic LITRPG Fantasy
Arcane Knight Book 4: An Epic LITRPG Fantasy

BIBLIOGRAPHY OF TIMOTHY MCGOWEN

THE ELEMENTAL REALMS

Nexus Guardian Book 1: A Fantasy LitRPG Adventure
Nexus Guardian Book 2: A Fantasy LitRPG Adventure

Journey To Crystal Mountain

The Crystal Mountain Saga Book 1

ISBN: 978-1-956179-25-5

First Edition: June 2023

Published By: Rising Tower Books

Publisher Website: www.RisingTowerBooks.com

Author Site: AuthorTimothyMcGowen.com

REVIEWS ARE IMPORTANT

Every review matters, get your voice heard.

Follow me on Amazon to get informed when my next book is released!

https://www.amazon.com/stores/Timothy-McGowen/author/B087QTTRJK

Join my Patreon for early Chapters!

https://www.patreon.com/TimothyMcGowen

Join my Facebook group and discuss the books

https://www.facebook.com/groups/234653175151521/

SPECIAL THANKS

I wanted to give a special thanks to those that helped bring this book to its current state.

Candace Morris - Alpha Reader, Beta Reader, Editor, and Proofer

I would also like to mention my patreons and thank them for their extra support!

Jesse Butcher, John Percival, Brad Gibson, Destin McMurray, Eric Letcher

Thank you.

I dedicate this book to all my nieces and nephews, good luck on the adventures of life.

CONTENTS

CHAPTER 1
NICE TO MEET YOU MR. SHADOW

-Zack-

"Good morning, class. My name is Mr. Shadow, and I will be your substitute teacher for today."

Glancing up from my comic book I saw who they had found to replace Mr. Philips. Standing behind the desk was a pale-skinned man with jet black hair slicked back with way too much hair gel. He was dressed like he was going to a funeral or maybe a fancy restaurant.

He wore a long black jacket over a stiff white shirt. I couldn't see from where he stood, but I imagined he had those shiny shoes to go with the getup. His name fit though, Mr. Shadow, he was creepy looking. His eyes were close set and surrounded by dark circles. The kind my mom gets when she has to work late too often. Will and

Owen were laughing at something a few desks over, probably a joke about Mr. Shadow. I strained my brain trying to come up with something to say first. I'd put a lot of work into being the class clown and couldn't afford to lose out now, so close to the end of the year.

"I didn't know they were letting corpses teach classes," I called out, cupping my hand in an attempt to throw my voice.

It didn't work and I knew that Mr. Shadow was on to me. But that was okay because I got a few chuckles. Jayden, Addy, and the snobby girl Sofia had all laughed. It wasn't my best joke, but I tried to take the good ones with the bad ones.

"And what is your name, jester?" Mr. Shadow asked, turning his full attention to me. His eyes seemed to burrow into his head as he looked in my direction.

"It isn't jester," I said, smirking. Again, I got a few laughs.

Mr. Shadow walked from behind his desk towards me. I was right, he had shiny shoes. They had a white stripe running down the sides, as did his pants.

Sunlight streamed in from the windows, but somehow Mr. Shadow was able to avoid it as he approached, slinking ever closer.

I changed my mind; he looked like he was late for a fancy dance. My eyes ran up and down the lanky man as he approached, looking for any more material to feed my jokes.

I found a few. He had an old-timey silver pocket watch; I could ask him where his monocle went. His legs were unusually long, perhaps he was related to a giraffe?

But I knew I was pushing my luck as he approached, a large vein on his forehead pulsed.

"Your name?" He hissed in a low nasally voice.

"Zack," I said, giving him a disarming grin in response.

"Well, Zack," Mr. Shadow said, emphasizing my name. "You and your laughing hyena friends have earned yourselves detention."

"Oh, come o-," I began to say but he slammed his hand down on my desk and I jumped. He wasn't allowed to do that, was he? I considered telling him as much, but my thought was cut off when Sofia spoke.

I looked over at her. She had curly dark auburn hair and olive-colored skin. When she spoke, it was with a slight Italian accent, but it was barely noticeable anymore. Now she had somehow adopted a 'rich girl who doesn't want to be talking to you' way of speaking that had a hint of her native tongue. Her parents had immigrated for business almost five years ago. They basically owned most of the town, my mom said.

"You don't mean to say that I also have detention, do you Mr. Shadow?" Sofia asked, her voice like sweet honey.

It made me almost laugh hearing her talk, she only spoke so nice when she wanted something. Otherwise, she was just demanding things in her usual terse tone and expected everyone to drop whatever they were doing and come to her aid.

"It does Indeed," Mr. Shadow said, his words were like a nasally snake that had learned to speak English. "Please enlighten me with your name, as well as you, and you." His finger pointed at Jayden and Addy.

After a few seconds of shocked silence, all three gave their names; Sofia, Addy, and Jayden-who looked most scared of all at the prospect of detention.

Jayden lived a few doors down from me and he helped me with my homework whenever I got a really hard assignment, which was like every single day this year. As far as I could remember, he had NEVER been given detention. His father was really strict about that stuff, always going on about how if he was going to be raising him all by himself, Jayden's mom passed away when we were in first grade, then Jayden had to do his very best just like his dad did.

"Now if we are quite done, let's start class," Mr. Shadow said. He walked to the front of the class and began writing math problems on the blackboard.

The rest of the day dragged on, and I didn't dare throw around anymore jokes. Even I understood that there was a limit to how far I could push someone.

"You really sunk my ship," Jayden said, sitting across from me at lunch.

"Who says that, dude?" I asked, trying to keep a smirk from my face; I failed.

"You think Einstein ever got detention?" Jayden asked, ignoring my question. He rubbed nervously at the back of his neck, while his Friday pizza—basically soft semi-soggy bread served with questionable toppings and half melted cheese—layed untouched on his tray.

"My brother, Landon, said Einstein failed out of school so if anyone is going to be like Einstein, it's probably me," I declared holding my head high, before taking a bite of my own oddly moist pizza square.

Jayden just gave me a half-hearted smile but didn't say anything, picking at the side of fruit with his plastic fork instead. I saw that he was wearing his 'cool Einstein' shirt again and felt a bit bad at declaring myself a closer match to Einstein. That stuff was important to Jayden and though I had many friends, I considered him my best friend.

"After today maybe you'll get failed out of school too," I said. But my words didn't seem to help his distressed mood and I couldn't figure out why.

Jayden readjusted his glasses, a thick black pair and the newest addition since I broke his last pair on accident. His

Dad was a barber, so Jayden always had the cleanest cut hair in the school, the sides shaved with cool lines sweeping back and tight curls on top. His brown eyes looked a tad too big due to his glasses, but I still thought he looked pretty cool.

"I can't do detention," Jayden declared suddenly. "I'm going to go to class early and see if I can convince Mr. Shadow to give me another chance."

As soon as Jayden declared this, he stood and took his tray of uneaten food, disposed of it and slipped out of the lunchroom.

Maybe he'd be able to convince him to get me out of detention too, because my mom was going to be super mad that I'd gotten my fifteenth detention. After the tenth one I'd had a meeting with the principal and my mom where she promised I'd behave more, which to be honest I didn't agree to. There was a promise of more meetings if I hit fifteen and sure enough I'd managed the difficult task in only two short months.

I really did try to do better, but I had a reputation to uphold. The title, 'Zack the Class Clown' wasn't going to earn itself. It wasn't my fault the teachers didn't have any sense of humor to speak of.

CHAPTER 2
I DON'T BELONG IN DETENTION

-Addy-

"Are you sure Principal Seymour isn't here?" I pleaded with Mrs. Johnson, the office secretary.

"I'm very sure Addison, now if you'd mind, I believe you are wanted in room 303 for detention."

"It's Addy," I shot over my shoulder as I left the office. I think Mrs. Johnson was saying something back, but I hurried away to join my classmates in detention.

It was wholly unfair that Zack had gotten us all in trouble. I had gone twelve years of my life without getting detention and at the end of my 7th-grade year BOOM, my flawless academic career was over.

My parents were NOT going to be happy when they heard about this. We had a plan and all I had to do was stick with it. My parents were both doctors and they expected me to be one too someday.

How was I going to get into any schools if I got labeled as some kind of delinquent!

Uhhhuuggh! It made me so mad. I stopped and stomped my foot. It was silly, but no one else was around so I allowed myself a little silliness.

The hallways were empty, everyone having already left for the day. Mrs. Johnson said our parents had been notified so I had no ride waiting for me outside.

A part of me wondered if I should just leave and walk home. I was already going to be labeled a misfit, a troublemaker, or a malcontent.

But no, what would my parents say?

Be strong and face the challenges that come your way. I said in my head mimicking my dad's deep serious voice.

Then I switched to my mom's sweet voice. There *will always be time to prove yourself honey, don't get worked up.*

Of course, they had already become doctors, they had nothing left to worry about.

The door to room 303 swung open just as I approached, and the lanky Mr. Shadow loomed over me.

"Welcome Addison, please come find your seat."

I opened my mouth to correct him but thought better of it. His voice sounded like a snake with a cold. Slithery and nasally at the same time. I couldn't help but grin as I walked past him, he really did look like a walking corpse.

No, stop that! That is what got you in trouble in the first place. I steeled myself and pressed my lips together.

Ahead in the desks sat my classmates.

Zack with his blonde wild hair and freckled face. He wore a red sweater and had the hood up. His blue jeans had a few small tears in them, he was always finding ways to rip them, either sliding through the dirt like he was playing baseball or wrestling with some of the older boys during recess.

Sofia wore her signature sour expression but smiled when she saw me, waving. We'd been on and off again friends for the past few years, currently on. I liked going to sleepovers at her place, it was really fancy. She wore a white top with a dark blue skirt and cute blue knee-high boots.

Sitting next to her and looking very nervous was Jayden. He had thick-rimmed black glasses, an 'Einstein with his tongue out' shirt, and a pair of khaki shorts. He had dark skin but strikingly light, amber-colored eyes.

He was good friends with Zack, but he really shouldn't be. I was sure Zack just used him for his brain.

He kept his black hair well-groomed, and the sides shaved close with little lines traveling the sides. I hadn't spent too much time hanging out with either Zack or Jayden in recent years, though, so I only knew what I had observed myself.

My dad told me it was always important to observe what was going on around me. He said it helped train your brain to notice things other people would miss and that would make me a better doctor.

It dawned on me that I would miss my oboe practice because today was Tuesday! It had been my Dad's idea at first to get me playing instruments and the oboe had been my idea. There was something to say about having an uncommon talent in an instrument.

My Dad told me that schools and scholarships loved that kind of stuff and despite my parents' profession I wouldn't consider us rich. My father ran a free clinic that only made a limited amount of money, I still wasn't a hundred percent clear how though.

I always dreamed of coming to work for them, but now that dream was in jeopardy. I frowned and sat down, glaring in Zack's direction. It was his fault for being a cute funny boy. Despite thinking the words in my head, I blushed a little, my annoyance subsiding for a few moments.

CHAPTER 3
THAT IS A MESSED-UP STORY

-Zack-

"You will not work on homework; you will listen to me. Is that understood?" Mr. Shadow announced to us after the last unlucky student arrived.

I couldn't believe he had given all of us detention. My joke wasn't even that funny, or at least that is what my mom said when she called to talk to me after school. I felt bad, she was going to be late to work now because she couldn't find someone to pick me up after detention and, according to her, it might cost her job. I wish she'd find a better paying job than the grocery store, so I wasn't too worried about her having to find a new job.

I took her advice and tried to tell Mr. Shadow about it all, but he didn't care.

"Why can't we work on homework," Addy said. I looked over in time to see her slowly putting her binder back in her pink backpack.

She was tall for our age, even taller than me and I was the tallest boy in our class. Her parents were doctors, something she liked to remind everyone about each chance she got. They ran a place in the more rundown part of town, a few blocks from where I lived. It was my mom's go-to place when one of us boys—I had four brothers, and I was the middle child—injured ourselves. So, we were basically there every other week.

Her hair was jet black with streaks of pink she'd added this year, and she wore a girly white shirt with a pair of neat blue jeans. We had grown up going to the same school in elementary and had even been friends for a time, but the last few years we'd grown apart. Now I admired her from afar. I tended not to worry about much, but girls were on my mind more and more.

"You have a problem following orders, Addison?" Mr. Shadow drew out her name like a snake's hiss.

I snickered. No one called Addy, Addison, she hated it. Sure enough, I saw her face go red and she let out a restrained breath of air.

"I don't, Mr. Shadow, sorry," Addy said, her words terse. She deflated in her seat.

Room 303 was on the west side of the school and the sun let several beams of light in, brightening the room.

The lanky Mr. Shadow did his best to avoid the light as he skulked through the classroom, taking his time to look at each of us.

His shiny dance shoes squeaked every time he turned, until finally, he spoke.

He ran his hands down his jacket and cleared his throat. "Did you know," he began. Then stopped to walk to the desk at the front of the classroom, sitting on its edge. "There is a place where kids go when they are unruly?"

"Isn't it called detention?" I blurted out.

Mr. Shadow glared in my direction.

"No, Zack." He drew out the words and focused on me. "This is child's play compared to the place that awaits you. And these questions are rhetorical, which means keep your mouths shut and listen. Far from the most distant corners of civilization there is an island unlike any other. It is a place untouched by mankind.

"Children are sent there and forced to learn how to survive. It is an island where the great dinosaurs still roam, where wild elemental magic is unleashed upon the unwitting, and where the impossible is possible!"

"Sounds awesome! When can we go?" I asked, laughing aloud. I put my feet up, I figured you couldn't get into much more trouble if you were already in detention, right?

I didn't know then how wrong I was.

"And you speak for your entire group?" Mr. Shadow asked, a grin splitting his face. "This is not a challenge to be taken lightly."

"Sure, yeah, why not," I said, "You guys ready to fight dinosaurs?"

No one answered, but Mr. Shadow must have taken their silence for an agreement.

"Then it shall be done," Mr. Shadow said. "An accord has been struck and a team assembled. Enjoy your challenge, vile children."

His words echoed in my head and the detention room began to spin and warp around me. I heard screams from all around, but I wasn't able to yell out myself. Instead, it was like my breath was stuck in my chest and if I didn't let it out soon the burning would be too much. Just when I couldn't possibly take another moment of it, the world went black, and all sound ceased.

The last thing I remember was the sensation of falling through an endless void of nothingness. I don't recommend it.

CHAPTER 4
ZACK, WHAT DID YOU DO?

-Addy-

So many responses had come to mind when Zack began being rude to Mr. Shadow, but I decided it was best I remain quiet.

When the room began to swirl though, I changed my mind.

"What is happening!" I screamed. I could see my classmates perfectly, but the rest of the room spun like a top. I fell out of the desk and tried to stand, but it wasn't possible. Someone turned the lights out and the ground beneath me gave way! I fell suddenly, until after only a few seconds I felt solid ground beneath me, and the lights had returned.

The beams of light coming in from the window were

brighter now and directly in my face. So, I stood and moved out of the way.

I then realized we were not in the classroom any longer, that much became crystal clear as soon as I looked up.

I was standing on the ground. It wasn't tiled floor any longer, but dirt. I realized that when I had moved the sun was being blocked by a huge tree that reached up into the sky. From the base of the tree, massive, gnarled roots broke the surface of the ground like limbs of an ancient kraken breaking the surface of the water. On my father's insistence I'd been expanding my reading and I'd recently finished a book on Nordic folklore.

I stood alone, my mouth and eyes hanging open in surprise as I scanned the area. It smelled nice outside, but that was hardly something worth mentioning. A gentle breeze brought the sounds of insects and birds.

A distant roar drained the color from my face.

A buzz and click caught my attention and I turned toward the noise.

Hanging from a lower branch was Cappy, the capuchin monkey that my uncle kept as a pet. The longer I studied it, doing my best to be observant, the more I realized this particular monkey was not actually Cappy.

For one thing, it appeared to be a robot of some kind. I approached slowly with my hand out to show I meant no harm. The monkey was hanging upside down by its tail and although the coloring was right, it didn't really have skin.

Instead, it was a mix of gears, metal rods, and overlapping colored plates that reflected light like a metallic sheen. It was a metal robot monkey!

Looking into its eyes I felt a bond, something clicked, and I could feel its thoughts. They weren't human thoughts that could be translated into words. No, they were just feelings and impressions.

For instance, I was getting a strong vibe that it wanted me to name it. As weird as today had been, I couldn't help myself.

"Can I call you Cappy?" I asked. It nodded vigorously at me, and I smiled. Through whatever strange bond we had I could feel that it thought of itself as Cappy now.

I lifted Cappy up, he was surprisingly light, and let him perch on my shoulder. Logically I knew I should be frightened or at least worried that I was in a massive jungle and had just made friends with a robotic monkey, but I felt a certain amount of calm being close to Cappy that was hard to process logically.

Cappy sent an urging for me to look at my arm, so I did. To my shock, there was some kind of thick copper band or bracelet on my right wrist. It had an odd language pressed into the surface all around and a circular slot could fit something round and flat. Despite being over four inches wide and a solid inch thick, I hadn't felt it before and even now didn't notice any weight or tightness from it.

It was on my right arm—which was good since I was left-handed. The metal or whatever it might be was a dull copper color with an odd golden sheen reflecting off it. It covered my forearm halfway between my wrist and elbow. No matter how I moved my arm it didn't feel like I was wearing anything at all.

I ran the bracelet across my face and felt a warmth from it. Then I tried to move it up or down my wrist and it began to itch, but not move. There was no place to unclasp the band and I couldn't help but freak out a little when I considered how it had gotten there.

I studied the engraved language again and tried to find any similarities between the three that I spoke. Not that I knew that many, just English, Mandarin, and Latin. My Latin was weak at best, but I'd worked hard over the several summers to improve.

As I studied the characters, I noticed that the golden sheen that appeared when light reflected from its surface showed a hidden layer of geometric shapes, barely noticeable and cut into the surface.

I reached out with my left hand and touched the surface again. To my surprise, all the geometric symbols— tiny traces in the metal—started giving off a faint white glow and a translucent white screen appeared in front of me. It was being projected from the band and stayed a foot above my forearm facing me.

Light Weaver: Level: 1, 0% Experience towards the next Level, 10/10 Charges Remaining.

As soon as I lifted my fingers off the gauntlet the words disappeared.

So, I was hallucinating that I'd entered some kind of game? Before I could fully process my thoughts and decide if that was in fact what had happened, I heard a scream cut through the trees around me.

My father's voice replayed in my head as it often did, *Help those you can when you can.* He wasn't a poet or anything, but very practical.

Without another thought, I ran toward the sound of the scream. I knew before I got there who it was, I'd heard Sofia scream plenty of times for one silly reason or another.

As I ran, it reminded me of those scary Jurassic Park movies, all the vegetation, trees included, were much bigger than they had any right being. I heard the gentle chirp of birds and the occasional buzz of bugs around me as I ran.

Finally, I made it around a sizeable tree and found Sofia. She was standing very still as a bug the size of a golden retriever slowly approached her, its wings buzzing here and there.

I couldn't know the bug's intentions, but I doubted that Sofia wanted to be that close to a critter that huge.

"Sofia!" I called out. "Are you okay?"

The bug must have been spooked by my voice as it lunged forward buzzing furiously towards Sofia. She screamed again and I reached out my arm toward her yelling her name.

A beam of light shot forth and struck the beetle. My right arm tingled, and I looked down at it in shock.

The beetle flew away immediately.

Running to Sofia's side I gave her a visual once over, no wounds, no visible trauma, okay she must be fine. Then I gave her a tight hug, she pushed me away after only a moment.

Sofia was staring at me as if I had some food stuck in my teeth or something.

"Was that a flashlight or something?" Sofia finally asked, getting over her initial shock.

"No, it came from this thing," I said, touching my right arm with my left hand. The display popped up again, but new information had been added.

Light Weaver: Level 1, 10% Experience towards the next Level, 9/10 Charges Remaining (59 Minutes, 48 Seconds till next Charge).

New Skill Unlocked! Beam of Light: Projects a beam of light from your **Soul Band***.*

I noticed the words 'Soul Band' was bolder than the rest and the moment I focused on it a bit harder, more information filled the display screen.

Equipped Item: Band of Suhtar, a device created by Suhtar at the height of his conquest. It can channel the power of Light in various ways. 9/10 Charges Remaining.

Focusing on the charges section I got even more info.

Band of Suhtar regains charges at a rate of 1 per hour.

"Oh my gosh, what is that gaudy thing?" Sofia asked, her words dragging me from my inspection. As I watched her, she looked down at her own arm and jumped in surprise.

On her arm was an identical forearm gauntlet, however, instead of a golden sheen when the light touched it, there was a white one. She scratched and clawed at it, but it refused to come off.

"Did you meet a robotic monkey too?" I asked, nodding my head towards Cappy. Things had gone so far off the rails that I was beginning to accept that this must all be a dream and I ought to just go with it until I woke back up in detention.

Sofia just then appeared to notice Cappy and shrieked again taking several steps backward.

"I hate monkeys," she cried.

Cappy turned around on my shoulder, putting his

face towards her. I could feel his emotions and he wasn't happy to be hated.

"What is happening!" Sofia shrieked, then putting her hand to her forehead she swooned and fainted. I rushed forward but I wasn't fast enough to catch her before she fell. Luckily she didn't hit her head. I helped to get her comfortable until she got over her bout of unconsciousness.

I kneeled on a rigid branch and felt very real pain. My pants had torn and suddenly I wasn't so sure this was a dream. The pain had felt all too real and even in my worst nightmares I'd never imagined myself in a video game, I didn't even play video games!

"Zack this is all your fault," I hissed between my teeth. Several things were becoming apparent to me at once.

First, this wasn't actually a hallucination, I would not have brought Sofia into my mind. Second, being in a jungle in the middle of nowhere was definitely going to put a damper on the plans my parents and I made for my future.

CHAPTER 5
COOL! A ROBOT BIRD!

-Zack-

I had a serious case of stomach pains so maybe I fell and hit my head? Yeah sure that made more sense than what I was seeing, this all had to be some sort of bad dream, right? I was alone in the woods, or maybe the jungle would be a better way to describe the massive plants and trees around me. The ground had giant finger like roots poking upward around a really green moss-covered tree.

Despite the dream that I was having, I enjoyed the smells, it was like that spray my mom liked to use when the room I shared with my youngest brother began to stink. Like a mix of evergreen and sweaty socks.

A pulling feeling washed over me suddenly and I

turned, facing the bright rays of sunlight that filtered through the trees. I heard a voice then and I jumped, but just as I turned away I felt an urging to go investigate.

I never considered myself brave really, but I was no chicken either. It wouldn't take more than a dare from any classmate, and I'd give something a try, no matter how stupid it might seem afterwards. So daring myself to go check out the voice, I shielded my eyes from the light with my hand and stepped forward.

Branches cracked under my feet, and after a few steps I sunk a few inches into the mud, nearly losing my badly tied left shoe. The voice sounded again and this time I heard it.

"Squawk! Seek the treasure. Squawk!"

On a branch at eye level was a grey bird that I recognized! It looked like the African Grey parrot my Dad had before he left.

"Ash? Is that you?" I asked, reaching out my hand. Ash was the best, he squawked a bunch which my dad never could train out of him.

Suddenly I wondered if I'd find my father here, I hadn't talked to him in months but last I'd heard he'd taken a job in Florida not the middle of a jungle.

As I looked at Ash I realized something odd, this definitely wasn't Ash...it was an odd collection of gears and metallic feathers made to look like a bird. The longer I looked at it the more I saw the robot bird and not Ash.

Despite this new revelation, I didn't withdraw my hand and a moment later it jumped onto my wrist. It was light and it walked over to sit on my shoulder, just as Ash had done.

"Squawk! Name me, name me! Squawk!"

At the same time it spoke I felt an impression or a deeper connection of some kind. I knew that it wanted me to name it, so I gave it a suitable name.

"You are Ash 2.0, but I'll just call you Ash," I declared, then added. "That work for you?"

"Squawk! Works for me! Squawk!"

I felt a calmness settle over me as Ash nuzzled behind my ear. Despite the strangeness of dreaming all this, it felt nice to have a connection to my father.

My left wrist itched, and I discovered another oddity. Someone had put girls' jewelry around my wrist. There was a thick bracelet sitting tight against my skin and I immediately tried to yank it off.

When I touched it with my right hand, a translucent white screen appeared before me with words floating right above the bracelet. I reacted by letting go of the slightly warm bracelet and the screen flickered away a moment later.

I hadn't gotten a chance to read any of the information. So slowly and carefully I reached out to touch the bracelet again. Just as before, a white translucent screen appeared, and I saw a blue sheen ripple over the bracelet.

My eyes flicked back to the screen, and I made sure to keep my hand pressed against the warmth of the copper-colored bracelet.

Creation Matrix: Level: 1, 0% Experience towards the next Level, 10/10 Charges Remaining.

After reading it all several times I removed my hand. Looking to the side and catching Ash's robotic orange eye I asked it a question.

"What is a creation matrix? I think I've heard of a movie called matrix but why is this bracelet named after a movie?"

"Squawk! Seek the treasure! Squawk!"

I got an urgent feeling from Ash along with his words, but I didn't know what to make of it. In the distance I thought I heard a scream, but I couldn't tell what direction. Then a moment later I heard a familiar voice not far off.

"Crap! Crap! Crap!" Jayden yelled running past a monstrous tree and right past me. Directly behind him was a miniature dinosaur! It ran on two feet and had a little head and small arms, but it wasn't even a foot tall.

No time to waste, I ran after the pair. It was my dream after all so I should have some of the fun. Jayden wasn't the most athletically inclined and his dino friend barely kept pace, which meant I caught up to the dinosaur within a few seconds.

It noticed me and lunged to the side, small jaw open

and showing a row of sharp needle like teeth. It bit my leg and pain jumped up my leg, causing me to stumble and fall. Before it could get another bite I reached down and smacked it in the head. This was enough to get it to release me and make a screeching sound before running off.

That hurt!

It got a part of my jeans that had already been torn and bit into my skin. Surprisingly it hadn't even broken the skin, leaving a line of red from the pressure only. If it had been any bigger that might have really been a problem.

Ahead, Jayden continued to yell and run like a mad man.

CHAPTER 6
WE NEED TO STAY CALM!

-Addy-

I helped Sofia up, but I was worried she was in shock or something, because her eyes were darting rapidly, and she wouldn't stop shaking.

"Sofia," I yelled. "Can you hear me!"

Her eyes locked on mine and her breathing came in rapid breaths. "Addy," she sounded scared. "What is happening?"

Cappy decided that would be a good moment to jump in her lap, Sofia screamed again and pushed him to the ground, scurrying to her feet. At least she wasn't freaking out anymore, sort of. The shaking and darting eyes had stopped, she just stood there with an angry look on her face.

"Wait until my daddy hears about this!" She yelled to no one in particular, while stopping her feet. I could relate to the foot stomping; I'd done a little of that already.

"So, you think it's real too?" I asked, getting up from where I'd been kneeling beside her. Cappy scurried up my leg and back to my shoulder.

"I'm not, like, dreaming," she said, shaking her head as if the thought of dreaming about being outside and in the dirt was appalling. "This place smells funny!" She said this last bit while beginning a new wave of whining sobs— these ones were definitely Sofia sobs though and those came and went depending on her mood, I knew this from experience.

I knew how to deal with these outbursts. Walking forward I wrapped Sofia in a warm hug and waited for her to stop. It took a whole two minutes before she emerged from my shoulder with red puffy eyes. Things were scary, we were alone in a strange place, and something had put a magical bracelet on my arm, but I had to keep it together for the both of us.

"It'll be okay," I lied, patting her back. "Someone will find us, and everything will be alright."

"Oh no!" Sofia screamed the words, her voice riddled with shock. I'd barely let her go a moment before and looked up to see what had happened now. She had lifted her left arm up and was staring right at her copper-colored bracelet, a wave of white reflective sheen traveled over it.

Please don't pass out, I silently begged her.

"It's fine," I said. "I don't know who put these things on us, but it helped already. Do you remember the big beetle and how I hit it with..." What had I hit it with, light? But that didn't make any sense, light couldn't hurt unless it was a laser or some powerful concentrated lens... "I don't know what with, but my point is, they can help! Touch yours and let's see what it says."

Sofia stomped her foot again. "I will do no such thing!" She yelled.

The surrounding sounds of birds and bugs went silent. "We probably shouldn't be so loud, I'm not sure what kind of predators are out here, but if that giant bug was any indication, we will be better off keeping a low profile."

Sofia glared at me, then at the trees, and then stomped her foot again, but didn't scream.

We stared at each other for several long seconds until Sofia finally cracked. She reached a trembling slow hand toward her bracelet and with the barest of touches activated it.

Spacer: Level 1, 0% Experience towards the next Level, 10/10 Charges Remaining

I read the display and frowned. "Focus on Spacer and see if it gives you any additional information," I said, trying to guide her to how I found more information.

Sofia scrunched her forehead in concentration then

only a second later let go of the bracelet and let out an exaggerated moan of frustration.

"It wooon't work," she moaned, folding her arms and sticking out her bottom lip.

I stepped up to her and put my hands on either side of her arm, forcing her to look me in the eyes. "I did it, so I know it will. Just focus on it and clear your mind, watch I'll try."

I pressed my hand against the bracelet and the information appeared.

Light Weaver: Level 1, 10% Experience towards the next Level, 9/10 Charges. (52 Minutes, 12 Seconds till next Charge).

Focusing on 'Light Weaver' I waited for additional information to appear. After a solid minute of trying, I let out my own huff of annoyed frustration. What in the heck!

"I'm waiting," Sofia said, moving her head back in forth like she did when she got impatient.

"I guess it doesn't always work," I said, deflating.

A series of yells echoed into the open area and Sofia jumped in surprise. I closed my eyes and focused on the location they were coming from, by the sound of it, another girl had been sent into the jungle with us.

"Who was that?" Sofia asked, pulling me back into a hug and holding me close more like a shield against whatever she was afraid of than for comfort.

I pulled myself free and locked on to the location it had come from. "Let's go, someone needs help!" I announced as I ran in the direction of the scream.

Sofia didn't follow at first, but after another scream and several foot stomps I heard her follow after me. I slowed my pace until she caught up, then went full speed into danger.

CHAPTER 7
SEVERAL THEORIES ON WHAT HAPPENED TO US

-Zack-

I caught up to Jayden just as he stopped in front of three of those skinny biting dinosaurs. When I put my hand on his shoulder he totally freaked out, turning and slapping his hands wildly toward me.

Stepping out of his wild attacks, I yelled at him. "Dude, relax! it's me, Zack!"

Jayden's glasses had been knocked askew and his eyes were wild. He finally seemed to see me, and he let out a breath.

"Zack! There are dinosaurs and I'm in a prehistoric jungle with plants that have been extinct for millions of years. This is my worst nightmare and my biggest dream all wrapped into one psychotic break," Jayden was speaking a mile a minute and when he finished, he turned and gestured to the small dinosaurs making weird mulling sounds at us. "Dinosaurs, Zack. We have dinosaurs!"

One of the small dinos lunged forward and I pushed past Jayden, catching it mid jump with my foot and punting it into a tree. It soared threw the air and hit the tree with a meaty 'thunk' before scurrying away, its two friends right behind it.

"Is this cool or what!" I said, petting Ash as he nuzzled into my ear. Jayden seemed to just take notice of Ash and he leaned forward, fascination plain to see on his face.

"It's a clockwork bird made to look like an African Grey right down to the eye color. This is most fascinating," Jayden said straightening his glasses and reaching out a finger. "I wonder what could be powering it? Does it require that you wind it up like a traditional clockwork construction or does it have some sort of internal mechanism, like a miniature motor?"

I didn't know the answer to any of these questions, but as soon as Jayden's finger was within a foot of Ash, the bird snipped its beak at him and spoke.

"Squawk! Back off Jack! Squawk!"

"My name is Jayden, not Jack," Jayden said, withdrawing his finger and leaning his head closer.

"Squawk! Jayden's gonna lose an eye! Squawk!"

That got his attention, and he took a whole two steps back.

"Sorry, Ash can be a bit rude," I said, smiling. This bird, despite being mechanical, reminded me so much of my dad's bird. It would say the funniest mean things just because it heard my dad say it.

"Do you think Mr. Shadow sent us here?" Jayden asked suddenly. He'd pulled out a little pocket notebook and was writing things down with a well-used pencil. "I was making a list of possible events that could have occurred to bring me to a new location without me realizing, but since you are here, I think we can assume a few of these don't fit. So, either we've been displaced by a temporal anomaly, been sucked into a wormhole, or Mr. Shadow used magic to send us to the island in his creepy story. Out of the three options, I'm inclined to want to believe the third, as a wormhole would surely have destroyed earth and a temporal anomaly could be literally anything."

I stared blankly at Jayden. He did this sometimes, speaking in a way I could barely follow. Like, who says things like 'temporal anomaly and wormhole'? It sounded like the reruns of star trek that my oldest brother likes to watch.

"Dude," I said, taking his little notebook and putting it in my pocket so he'd look at me. "This can't be real. Maybe we are sharing a dream while sleeping in detention? You know anything about that, like shared experience mental stuff?"

Without his notebook taking up his attention, Jayden realized he had a copper bracelet on his arm and had taken to poking it with his pencil. As I watched, a sheen of green color passed over it, Jayden must have saw it as well because he dropped his pencil in shock.

Ever so slowly he reached out with his left hand to touch the bracelet, but I couldn't help myself.

"Oh no!" I screamed loudly.

Jayden jumped so much that he actually fell over. I broke out into a laughing fit, but he didn't look amused at all, which for some reason made me laugh harder.

"You have one too!" Jayden said, seeing mine tightly wrapped around my left wrist. "But it's on the opposite wrist, look, mine is on my right wrist, I wonder if that has to do with me being left-handed. I know you are right-handed, so it seems like a plausible hypothesis."

Picking up his pencil, he held his hand out and I gave back his notebook. He began to write notes again until finally I cleared my throat.

"Check this out," I said, touching my hand to my copper band.

Creation Matrix: Level 1: 1, 0% Experience towards the next Level, 10/10 Charges Remaining.

Jayden's eyes went wide as he read the information on my white translucent screen.

"It's a hologram projection! But how do the lights make a readable surface and why does it look like I'm staring right at it no matter how I move my head?" Jayden shot off questions as he walked around me and kept his eyes on the screen. Reaching forward he poked it with his hand, but it passed right through without disturbing the image.

"Pretty cool, right!" I said, feeling good about showing off.

Jayden just nodded his head before scribbling more notes and turning the page of his pocket notebook. Then, as if something occurred to him, he put his notebook and pencil away and touched his own copper band.

A screen appeared just as it had with mine, but his read slightly differently.

Bondsmith: Level 1, 0% Experience towards the next Level, 10/10 Charges Remaining.

"Bondsmith," Jayden said, rubbing at the back of his neck nervously. "Why do I feel like I've read that term before. Must be in one of the hundreds of books I read last summer. What do the words mean, 'Creation Matrix' and 'Bondsmith'? Have you been able to determine what a creation matrix does?" Jayden turned his attention back to me and I shook my head.

"I came running after you like 2 seconds after finding the thing stuck to my arm," I said, raising my hands up in an 'I don't know' gesture. "But you're the one with the huge head, you tell me how they work."

Jayden smiled, I teased him often, but we were friends

and he always brightened when I joked about how smart he was. It wasn't like I had to stretch the truth much, he was literally the smartest guy I knew and that included the teachers and my mom. It was like everything to do with school and learning just came as easy to him as goofing off came to me.

"Right so I'll start by seeing if I can interact with the hologram, perhaps voice commands, or gestures of some kind," Jayden had his notebook out again and writing away. Just as he pressed his copper band, a sound of ruffling leaves and footsteps came from behind a wall of green plants.

It was my turn to shine. I took up a defensive posture, ready to kick away more tiny dinosaurs, Jayden shrunk behind me and I could hear him still scribbling away on that notebook.

Then something much bigger than a tiny dino broke through the brush.

CHAPTER 8
TO THE CAVE!

-Addy-

J ust as we pushed ourselves through the thick vegetation, screams filled the area. The surprise of it made me scream, and then Sofia began to scream until everyone was screaming. Surprise fright turned into sudden realization as I saw who stood before us.

"Jayden! Zack! You're here too?" I asked, as all the screams subsided and everyone came to realize that it was just us, the detention crew back together again.

"Addy?" Zack asked, then switching his gaze to Sofia. "Sofia? How'd you guys get into this dream?"

"It isn't a dream! Have you noticed these things?" I asked, holding up the bracelet and pressing my hand to it.

The display appeared, but they didn't seem nearly as shocked as I expected.

"Like video game stats, right?" Zack asked, nudging Jayden as if he were in on some joke that I wasn't. Jayden jumped a little, he looked like he was on the verge of having a mental breakdown, sweat pouring down his forehead and his eyes flipping around at nothing.

But suddenly he focused on me and spoke. "I've tried a few methods of interacting with the hologram, but so far nothing," Jayden said, putting a hand on his own and summoning forth the display.

"I've got it to respond to my thoughts," I said, then added, "Once at least."

"Can this horrid shared nightmare please end," Sofia said, clasping her face between her hands.

Jayden ignored her and scrunched his brow in concentration as he tried my method.

"Band of Suhtar?" Jayden said, tilting his head to the side in confusion. "I have 10 out of 10 charges, but I'm unsure what it does? Mine is called 'Bondsmith' and Zack's said 'Creation Matrix' what do yours say?"

I tapped my chin, remembering what Sofia's said, then answered. "Mine is 'Light Weaver' and Sofia's is 'Spacer'."

"Because she spaces out in class, right?" Zack said, a lame attempt at humor that didn't earn him any laughs.

Before he could try again, which it looked like he might, I added, "I unlocked a skill called 'Beam of Light'.

It basically allowed me to shoot light at a giant beetle. Have you guys seen any other huge insects?"

"Zack saved me from a Compsognathus," Jayden said matter-of-factly.

I'd heard that name before and it only took a few seconds for it to click. "You mean a dinosaur!" I basically shouted the words as the new layer of 'we are in big trouble' settled over me.

"It was pretty small," Jayden said.

"Not that small," Zack interjected, kicking at an exposed root in the ground.

"Size doesn't matter!" Sofia screamed. "You are saying a freaking DINOSUAR attacked you? I want my daddy..." Sofia went from screaming in red faced anger to sitting down again on a tree and repeating that she wanted her daddy.

I recognized the signs and knelt beside her, wrapping her with my arms. "It'll be okay, we will figure it out."

I didn't think it would be that easy, but Sofia nodded, wiped away a few tears and stood.

"We need to find shelter while we wait to be rescued," Sofia announced, lifting her chin. I knew she was used to getting her way and most of the time I ignored her small commands, but in this case she had a good point.

"Yeah, follow me, I'm a boy scout and I'll find us a cave or something," Zack announced, not waiting for any responses he marched off in what I was sure had to be a random direction.

Jayden turned, putting away his little notebook, and hurried after his friend. I barely made out what he said next, but it made me smile. "You haven't come to boy scouts this entire year, I thought you quit?"

"Quiet," Zack shot back, looking over his shoulder and smiling.

Sofia broke first, letting out a frustrated huff of air and stomped after them, then with a sigh of my own I followed, taking a spot in the back.

We'd been walking for ten minutes when we passed through an opening in the trees, one huge tree had fallen on another creating a triangular doorway of sorts. Of course, Zack took us straight through. On the other side was a large open space and on the far end a cave opening big enough to park a house inside.

"Found a cave!" Zack announced, like we couldn't see the enormous opening across the way.

"Okay boy scout," I said, hurrying up to him. "How do we know if it'll be safe inside? Caves are homes to all sorts of animals."

"We can just hang out in the front for now," Zack said shrugging. "If we hear anything we'll run."

"Genius plan!" I said sarcastically.

Zack beamed, smiling wide and answered with a confident. "Thank you."

Uhg. Why were boys so frustrating. Even Jayden, the smart one, didn't protest, instead he followed Zack right up to the edge of the cave and sat beside him on a flat rock.

Doing my best not to lose it like Sofia had, I searched the area for any signs of danger. The ground around the cave was all rocks, so it was impossible to see any tracks, but I did make a surprising find at the edge of the cave wall. Water trickled down from higher up someplace into a natural cut bowl.

Sofia followed my gaze, walking beside me as I searched, and exclaimed in surprise. "Water!" Before leaning down and taking a cup full into her hands, drinking it down before I could protest.

"Is that water clean?" Zack asked while I tried to search for the right way to tell Sofia that she'd probably just ingested any amount of unknown bacteria.

"It's the best water I've ever tasted!" Sofia declared, going for another handful.

"Its running down from the mountain, probably melting from snow above," Jayden added, taking out his notebook and making notes. "The human body requires a substantial amount of water, but I'd suggest we wait to see what effect it has on Sofia before the rest of us consume any." He spoke very robotic and matter-of-factly.

"You feel sick yet?" Zack asked, just as Sofia was about to take her third handful of water.

"Uh, no, gross," Sofia said, slurping up more water.

She finished and wiped her hand on her pants then straightened her shirt.

"Tell me if you feel anything out of the ordinary," I said, giving in to Jayden's plan. He was right that we needed water and that since Sofia had already drank some, we ought to just wait and make sure she was safe.

"Squawk! Seek the companions! Squawk!"

I jumped and looked at the little robotic bird on Zack's shoulder, how had I not really noticed it till now?

"You got one too?" I asked, gesturing to Cappy who sat on my shoulder.

Zack blinked several times, as if seeing him for the first time as well.

"Where did the monkey come from?" He asked, standing up suddenly.

"Interesting," Jayden said, scribbling away. "I looked at you many times but only now am I seeing the clockwork monkey. Maybe there is some advanced science at work here. Could be like Doctor Who where it has a filter of our ability to perceive it, a perception filter."

Jayden was going full geek mode, walking right up to Cappy and poking him with his pen. I could sense that Cappy didn't mind but felt something else. The bird's words echoed in my head.

"We need to find your companions," I said, looking from Jayden to Sofia. I didn't know how I knew this, but I felt it like a fact pressing into my mind. "I can't say why but I just feel like we need to do it and soon."

"I feel the same thing," Zack said, shaking his head. It wasn't often I'd be relieved to have Zack agree with me, but here we are, and I was.

CHAPTER 9
CRAFTING IS EPIC!

-Zack-

I t was getting darker, what little light there was could be seen through the trees fading with each passing minute.

"We should start a fire, I can feel it getting colder already," I said. None of us were wearing clothes meant for cold weather and while it hadn't gotten *that* cold, soon it would be so dark that we'd be unable to see anything.

My desire to crack jokes and make fun of the situation we were in was rapidly decreasing as the reality of it sunk in. We were alone, in the wild, and all by ourselves. Jayden was right of course; I had dropped out of the boy scouts. I couldn't even remember how to make a fire, but I knew I needed wood.

"Help me get some wood," I told Jayden, he adjusted his glasses and stood, ready to follow me into anything. Jayden was a good friend, and I was glad I had him at my side.

Addy talked with Sofia, rubbing her back and probably listing off all the ways she would get sick. Addy knew stuff like that because her parents were doctors. I tried to think about what I knew because of my parents but stopped that line of thinking before it went too far. I loved my parents, and they'd taught me plenty, just not doctor stuff.

The wood we found felt damp, but we collected a good arm full each anyways. There were sounds all around us, chirps of birds and bugs, the occasional breeze setting the greenery moving around us, but no dinosaurs. Not yet at least. As we gathered up the wood to prepare, I tried to think of a way out of our situation.

If this were all real then we could make a bon fire and that would alert grownups to where we are, or maybe we'd burn down the forest and get stuck, unable to escape. This wasn't my strong suit, figuring out escape plans, I was more of jokes guy. It wasn't that I felt out of place in the middle of a forest, my dad had taken be hunting a few times and we'd even killed a deer once, so I knew my way around a forest.

"I found a few flint rocks, but I don't think this wet wood will light. We need something dry as a starter,"

Jayden said, doing a way better job at knowing all the boy scout stuff than me.

"Can't we just rub two sticks together, like on the cartoons?" I asked, taking one of the rocks he'd picked up and wondering how he knew it was flint.

"That requires dry wood and I've only ever seen it done once," Jayden said, looking apologetic like any of this was his fault.

"Okay, here, let me handle this," I said, taking the other rock and trying to remember how to do it.

I smacked the rocks together and saw the tiniest of a spark, but the wet wood refused to light. I pictured in my head what I wanted, a blazing campfire and tried again.

Suddenly, I felt something build up inside of me and then warmth blossomed beneath me. I jumped back as the flames of a perfectly made campfire nipped at me.

"How is that possible!" Addy said, getting to her feet and looking at me like I was some kind of unknowable monster.

"I...I was just picturing what I wanted, like my mom always tells me, picture what you want and do your best, I never thought it'd work so well!" I exclaimed, my words rolling out as I tried to make sense of what I'd done.

"Touch your bracelet," Addy said, shaking her head knowingly.

Creation Matrix: Level 1, 25% Experience towards the

next Level, 9/10 Charges Remaining (59 Minutes, 45 Seconds till next Charge).

New Crafting Branch Unlocked! The Basics: Through the power of your **Soul Band,** *you can now do* **<u>Basic Crafting Recipes</u>.**

I read it all and a huge smile grew on my face. I'd played games that had crafting before, and I loved it! Things were about to get way better for us, I hoped.

"Focus on the basic crafting recipes and see what appears," Addy said, and I did my best to follow her advice.

Focusing on it, more information appeared on the display.

<u>Basic Crafting Recipes</u>: *Campfire, Torch, Moss Bedroll, Linen.*

"Whoa, this is cool! What's linen?" I asked, trying to remember where I'd heard of it before.

"Basically, like cloth but made with plants instead of wool," Sofia said, surprising us all. She saw us looking and shrugged. "I know a thing or two about clothing, so sue me."

"So, I can make a campfire, a torch, a moss bedroll, and clothing?" I asked no one in particular. "Should we try to collect moss to make some beds?"

"I saw a great deal, but it has gotten pretty dark," Jayden said, looking at the dark surroundings with apprehension.

"I'll make a torch," I offered, grabbing a few pieces of the wood the campfire hadn't sucked up and focused on picturing a torch like from the games I played. I felt something build up inside of me, but it fizzled out before anything happened. "It didn't work," I said.

"Maybe you're missing something," Addy said. "I doubt torches are made up of just wood. Did you focus on the recipe and see if anything else was required?"

I shot Addy a look, of course I didn't. Placing my hand back on the copper band I focused on the Basic Recipes then on the Torch.

Torch: Requires 1x Wood, 1x Linen or Moss or Cotton.

"See, what did I tell you," Addy said, marching up to me. I eyed her suspiciously and rightfully so, because she reached out and ripped my sleeve right off. "Here is your cotton."

"I liked this shirt," I complained, still dumbstruck at what she'd done. A part of me stirred and a thought came unbidden to my mind. 'I like Addy.' Come on mind! Now is not the time for those thoughts, I pushed away the stray thoughts and focused on using my sleeve to make the torch.

With the wood and the cotton, I felt everything click into place and suddenly I was carrying a burning torch.

Getting the moss took no time at all and soon we were back in the safety of our cave, where the fire continued to burn warmly. I discovered a few things while trying to make the Moss bedrolls, first, I end up getting a bunch of large leaves and turned them into linen, neat little piles of it. Then with the linen and moss collected I was finally able to make four bedrolls, basically moss sleeping bags with linen liner inside. Crafting the additional 8 items earned me enough to hit level 2!

I didn't know what that meant or how it affected my crafting, but it reset my charges and it gave me five more to work with, which was good because I'd run out after making the last bedroll.

Creation Matrix: Level 2, 5% Experience towards the next Level, 15/15 Charges Remaining

We all went to bed shortly after, our bedrolls lined up next to the fire. Despite being hungry and thirsty, I was extremely tired and went to sleep almost immediately.

CHAPTER 10
THAT'S A FOX!

-Addy-

I watched as Zack strutted around in the morning, turning plants into linen as if the process was that easy. His bracelet had some kind of magic in it that just poofed items to completion.

"You know," I said, feeling a tad jealous but doing my best to keep it from my face, "my bracelet shoots out laser beams."

"Really!" Zack exclaimed. He stopped turning piles of greenery to linen and came over. Jayden had his notebook out again and looked intrigued as well. "Can we see?"

I looked at Zack, then to Jayden, both looked so excited that I figured I might as well. Sofia laid in her bedroll still, pretending to be asleep.

I shrugged, what harm could it do?

Walking just outside the cave, I took aim at the nearest tree and focused on the name of the ability. Nothing happened. Getting a touch panicked that perhaps I wouldn't be able to show off after all, I shook my arm a bit.

Come on stupid arm thing, work!

Then I had an idea. Instead of focusing on the ability, I focused on how I felt when I saw Sofia in need of help. I couldn't quite muster the same feelings, but I came close. The morning light was still pretty dim and for a second I kept thinking about how dark it was compared to the first time I'd used the ability.

Suddenly, I felt a whoosh come over me and my bracelet went off. But instead of a beam of light smashing into the tree, something else happened.

A globe of light hovered beside me brightening the space between the cavemouth and the tree line. I checked my bracelet and saw that I had learned a new skill!

New Skill Unlocked! Globe of Light: Summons a ball of hardened light that will follow you for ten minutes before dissipating.

"That wasn't a laser," Zack said, not at all sounding impressed by my new skill. I'd summoned light, which meant we didn't need his burning torches anymore, he was probably jealous.

"Was that a new feature you unlocked, or have you

always been able to make balls of light?" Jayden asked, scribbling away at his notebook. The little thing had to be getting close to full already.

I smiled, happy that someone was interested in my new skill. "Just learned it," I admitted. "I'm still working out how to activate my skills and I stumbled on a new one while trying to use my 'Beam of Light' skill."

"Can you try to do the beam one again?" Jayden asked, his nervousness all but gone as he got more excited about witnessing more abilities.

"I can try," I said, holding out my arm again.

I focused on the name, then with a sudden burst of inspiration, I pictured what I wanted it to do. Suddenly I felt something build up inside of me and a beam of light shot from my hand, leaving a scorch mark on the tree. A tiny tendril of smoke traveled up from the spot I hit, but no fire.

"Whoa, that's cool!" Zack said, walking right up to me. He held his hand up like he was going in for a high-five, so I gave him one. It was satisfying to be the center of attention for once, with a friend like Sofia in school it meant no one ever spent much time looking at me.

I didn't need that, I reminded myself, my parents and I had a plan, and that plan would get me where it truly mattered. But now, out here in the middle of who knows where, I felt a measure of that pressure lessen as well. For once in my life maybe it would be alright to just wing it and be free.

"Can you tell me what you did to make it work this time?" Jayden asked, his pen ready to write.

"Sure thing," I said, smiling. "I focused on what I wanted to do, pictured it in my mind and it worked."

"Hey! That is how I do it too, I have to focus on what I want to happen before it'll kick in," Zack added. Behind us, Sofia had finally gotten out of bed.

"Based on all the data, I think I am ready to theorize what my copper band is capable of," Jayden announced, closing his little notebook and adjusting his glasses.

Jayden picked up two rocks and squeezed his forehead into a line, his eyes as focused as they could be. Then he let go of one of the rocks and the other fell to the ground. "Dangit, I really thought that'd work. I mean, it says 'Bondsmith', so I thought maybe I'd be able to bond things together. So much for that theory."

"What about mine?" Sofia asked, yawning. "What does spacer even mean? Like, it'll take me out into space or something?"

"Nah, it means you are a total space-case," Zack said. He was the only one that laughed.

I walked up to Sofia and put a hand on her back. "I'm sure we will figure it out, we just need a little time."

Jayden was lost in his notes again, but suddenly he stiffened and looked out into the trees. He didn't say anything as he put his notebook away and kept staring forward as if something had caught his attention.

"I'm hungry," Sofia complained. "Where's breakfast?"

Jayden seemed to get knocked out of whatever trance he was in and spoke up, his nervous tone responding to her. "I've studied various edible and poisonous berries, maybe we can collect some food out there." He pointed in the direction he'd been staring. It was a different part of the jungle that we'd not been in yet.

"We can run the juices on our skin and see if there is any reaction before we eat one," I suggested. I think that was meant for testing if you were allergic, but maybe it applied to poison berries as well.

In a group—Zack in the lead, followed by Jayden, with Sofia and I in the back—we went looking for food.

We found berries, Jayden identified them as Huckleberries and warned that while edible, it might be best to boil them to clean them off. Zack announced that he would try to cook them over the fire with his crafting skills, and to keep an eye out for rocks that could be used as either a bowl or plate.

We'd collected several pockets full of Huckleberries and then came upon some Cloudberries, we were so hungry that we took a chance and ate them raw. We all had stomachs filled with the juicy tart orange and red berries.

Just as we decided to turn back, Jayden ran off ahead,

something that surprised us all. I pushed back a confused Zack and caught up with Jayden some dozen feet ahead.

He was kneeling down beside a silver fox. At first I didn't see it, but it was hard to mistake it as Jayden picked it up and let it sit on his shoulder. I saw then that it was mechanical and knew that he'd just found his own companion. Cappy leaned forward as if he was greeting our newest member of the team.

Jayden turned with a huge smile on his face. "I'd like to introduce you all to 'Neil deGrasse Tyson', my pet fox. You can just call him Neil."

"Hey, you found your own little buddy!" Zack said, coming up to stand beside me.

"Squawk! Welcome to the club! Squawk!"

Neil, who had the coloring of a silver fox and looked far more robotic than the rest of our companions so far, tilted its head toward Zack's bird, Ash, acknowledging it. I felt Cappy's reaction as well, he was pleased to have another of his kind nearby.

"Can we talk about these robots that keep showing up?" Sofia asked, she had taken several steps away from the group and had her hands up in front of her.

"They're just our friends," I said, shaking my head. Why was she so worried about Cappy and his friends? I knew without being told that they weren't dangerous, they were meant to be at our sides, like helpful guides.

I stopped suddenly and went over my thoughts. Why

had I been so ready to accept the companionship of a robotic monkey that reminded me of a pet I used to know? But any sense of strangeness faded away as I felt a wave of calm settle over me from Cappy. I smiled, content with how the situation had worked out so far.

CHAPTER 11
I CAN CRAFT FOOD?

-Zack-

We got back to our makeshift camp, three of us now with cool side-kick robot pets. Sofia must be jealous or something, because she was moping around in the mouth of the cave, not saying much. I tried to go over and tell her a few jokes about Ash and the others, but I don't think it helped. I guess pretending that Ash had taken over my body and speaking like the bird wasn't the way to go.

With my charges at half, I tried to figure out how to cook the berries I had collected. Between what we all had in our pockets, there was a good-sized pile and I'd found a thin rock that would work well enough as a bowl. Using the water, Sofia hadn't gotten sick yet so we decided it must be good water, I filled the bowl then began to add berries.

The fire was going again, so using a forked stick I'd found, I held the rock bowl over the fire, hoping I'd be able to boil them or something. While doing so, I focused on what I wanted to happen, 'cook the berries' I repeated in my head. I felt a whooshing from my arm and looked back at the plate. The water was gone and, in its place, was a dark blue juice.

Using my free hand, I touched my copper band to see what the heck I'd just done.

New Crafting Branch Unlocked! Cooking: Through the power of your Soul Band, you can now do Cooking Recipes.

Cooking Recipes: Huckleberry Juice.

"Hey guys, I made juice!" I called out, moving the stone bowl closer and testing the surface temperature with my hand. It was ice cold, which seemed strange considering I'd just had it over a fire. Taking a sip of the juice I found it very sweet with a slight tartness to the flavor and extremely cold.

"Whoa you can cook things now too?" Jayden asked, taking a few notes as he inspected the juice.

"How does it taste?" Addy asked. I could tell she was thirsty, as she was the last holdout to try the water. I held the bowl out to her, teasingly taking it back as she reached for it.

"Just kidding, it's really sweet! Try some," I said,

holding it out again. I was tempted to pull it away again, but I could tell Addy was pretty thirsty, so I let her take the bowl.

At first, she just gave it a tentative sip, but after tasting it she downed the entire bowl's worth of juice. I heard her stomach gurgle and for some reason I immediately tried to think of other things I might be able to cook. If we could capture a bunny or something, my dad had shown me how to skin them and take the guts out. I'd only done it once, but I was sure I could do it again.

Then I remembered we'd need a knife for that and I got a wonderful idea.

"I'm going to craft a knife!" I declared, looking through the stones to find one that was long enough. The best I found was an oval rock twice as long as my grip was wide. A rock knife wouldn't be the best, but if I could somehow sharpen it and give it a handle wrap, it would work.

I grabbed some of the linen and wrapped it to make a little handle, it wasn't perfect, but it might work. Then I began to run it across another larger rock to knock off bits. The way I figured it, I should get it as close to what I wanted before I tried to use my cool skills. I felt Ash agree with my thoughts and kept on task.

In the middle of giving the makeshift knife a subtle edge, Jayden stood over me.

"Do you think making a knife is a good idea?" He asked, his voice had his usual nervous cadence to it.

"Step one is make a knife," I said, not taking my eyes off my task. "Step two is finding a bunny or something to kill, maybe that will be step three because I need to make a trap or something to catch it. What I'm saying is, I have a plan."

"Be careful," Jayden said, I looked up to see him wringing his hands.

"It'll be alright, trust me dude," I said, smiling and showing him my makeshift knife.

He stepped back and said, "Careful."

I went back to work, focusing my mind on what I wanted it to look like and I felt a whooshing leaving my arm and run into the knife. I crafted a knife!

Creation Matrix: Level 2, 69% Experience towards the next Level, 5/15 Charges Remaining.

New Crafting Branch Unlocked! Basic Stone Tools: Through the power of your Soul Band you can now do Basic Stone Tool Recipes.

Basic Stone Tools: Crude Stone Axe, Crude Stone Knife, Crude Stone Pickaxe, Crude Stone Machete

I could make a machete! Wasn't that basically a sword? Oh, this was getting really cool. I focused on the machete and saw that it required five stone, wood, and linen or leather. Gathering up the materials I began to work on the wooden handle, as I saw no way to turn the stones I had into a sword of any kind. When I had a rough shape of a handle, only having nearly cut my hand a few times, I focused on picturing what I wanted.

Another whoosh later and I had a stone sword, or technically a machete, but it was awesome all the same. It didn't look like I expected or tried to picture, instead of a long stone blade sharpened to a point, it extended the wooden handle into bat length and added the stones in between tied into place with the linen. Only one side had the rocks sharpened to a point and to me it looked more like a strange bat and axe mixed together, but what did I know.

"You made a very crude looking Macuahuitl!" Jayden said, sounding very surprised.

"Mawkawit?" I asked, attempting and failing to say whatever Jayden had said.

"Yeah, used in Mesoamerica by the Aztecs and others during that time period. Normally I think both sides have sharpened obsidian, but yours looks passable!" Jayden said, he seemed very excited but also wouldn't get any closer to look at it.

I stepped back just to be extra safe, but mostly because I didn't want to keep scaring Jayden, and then I gave it a few swings. I was no baseball star, but I'd swung a bat plenty and this felt no different. Setting it aside, I went to work on making a simple trap, using a flat rock, a makeshift rope from the linens, and a stick to hold up the rock, it wasn't going to catch much, but if something knocked the stick over and the rock fell on them, maybe I could get us meat.

I learned a new branch of crafting called 'Traps', and my trap was just named, Simple Snare. I also learned to make rope, along with my Basic Crafting Recipes, which was nice. I hit level three, and my Charges reset as well as went up to 20 out of 20.

Creation Matrix: Level 3, 5% Experience towards the next Level, 20/20 Charges Remaining.

It was midday now and I'd kept busy enough that I didn't notice Addy and Sofia had taken off on their own someplace.

"Where'd the girls go?" I asked, walking up to Jayden. He was trying to stick things together still, but nothing had worked yet.

"Left to get berries, they said they wouldn't go far, and I volunteered to stay behind to watch you," Jayden said distractedly, while holding a stone and wood together.

"I don't need someone to watch over me," I declared, resting the swordbat on my shoulder and scratching my neck with it on accident. Ouch, that hurt.

CHAPTER 12
I DON'T EVEN LIKE SNAKES...

-Addy-

I know it shouldn't matter, so many other things were important, like how on earth we'd get our way home, but it did. Zack was leveling up much faster than me and I wanted to change that. As soon as we left, I began putting up globes of light, watching my experience slowly tick upward until I too, hit level 2.

Sofia kept sending me worried looks, but I knew she was just having trouble with our companions, surely she'd find hers soon. They were so helpful, whenever I worried too much, I felt Cappy gently soothing my worries.

We picked berries as we went, careful to only grab the kind that Jayden identified as safe. He was a pretty cool guy, Jayden. So smart and resourceful, I can't imagine what we'd be doing if he hadn't been sent along with us. Then there was Zack, the foolhardy, goofy kid and the only reason we were here in the first place. No, that wasn't fair, I felt Cappy soothe my emotions.

Zack couldn't have known or controlled any of this, so it wasn't right for me to blame him. He was pretty cool when I thought about it, and I did laughed at his joke, as dumb as it might have been.

My balls of light did little to illuminate an already bright afternoon. The vegetation looked like it was pulled straight from a dinosaur movie, over-sized leaves and huge trees. But interspersed between it all were plants like the ones we found berries on, normal and mundane looking things. As I let my mind wander, I landed on a topic that bothered me.

How had we really gotten here? It was magic, wasn't it? These bracelets were magic, and magic had transported us here, so maybe magic could get us back. But where would we find the magic we needed to get back?

More questions than answers occurred to me, when suddenly Sofia jumped beside me, catching my attention.

"A snake!" She yelled, hiding behind me and peeking at it. I scanned the ground looking for what she'd seen, but it wasn't until I looked practically at my feet that I saw it.

The snake was yellow, but little silver gears could be seen under the yellow plates as it slithered back and forth.

There was no doubt in my mind when I looked at it, that this was another companion, so why was Sofia afraid of it.

"It looks just like my brother's snake!" She screeched. "I hate that thing; he always torments me with it! Stupid snake, he even named it after a boy I liked. Cory the snake. As if! But I guess you aren't so bad." She suddenly changed her tone and reached down to the snake. It slithered up her arm and to my surprise she didn't flinch back.

"Not sure why I was so worried about these little guys," Sofia said, making kissy faces at the snake. "They aren't so bad."

And just like that all four of us had robotic animal companions.

CHAPTER 13
MORE DINOSAURS!

-Zack-

Jayden and I decided to mount a search and rescue after hearing a scream coming from the jungle. We made it a ways out when we encountered Addy and Sofia.

Sofia had a snake on her shoulder, meaning we'd all found our companions now. Snakes were cool and I went right up to Sofia, ignoring the nasty look she shot me and stuck my finger out at the snake. It hissed, matching the tone of Sofia's glare and I stepped back, alarmed.

"Hey, tell your snake to chill," I said, holding my hand close to me, as if it were in danger.

"Stay out of our bubble, clown boy," Sofia said. If she

knew me better, she'd know that wasn't an insult to me at all, in fact I loved being the class clown, so there.

I held back an urge to stick my tongue out and decided to try my hand at a snake joke.

"You and your snake slithered out of the same hole, didn't you?" I asked. Darn that wasn't really funny, let's see, what is funny about snakes...

"Hey, Sofia," I said, finally coming up with something.

"What?" She asked, completely deadpan.

"What do snakes use to measure?" I asked, but before she could answer I delivered the punchline. "Inches, because they don't have feet!"

Addy and Jayden chuckled, and I felt vindicated. Another joke came together, one I'd read in a joke book once before.

"How do venomous snakes kill?" I asked, then like before, I hit her with the punchline before she could respond. "In cold blood!"

Jayden laughed, Addy grinned, and Sofia scowled.

Still got it, I told myself, walking past Sofia.

"We came to help," Jayden said when he finished laughing. "Who screamed?"

"It was Sofia," Addy said, yawning. She stretched out her arms and her monkey hugged her neck.

Did I know any good monkey jokes? While I went over a few that came to mind, Ash spoke.

"Squawk! Seek the Treasure! Squawk!"

"If you throw a monkey into salty water what will it become?" I asked, standing in front of Addy. Before she could answer I gave the punchline. "Wet."

This time I started laughing hysterically, but I couldn't tell if anyone else found it funny. Wiping a tear away I got control of myself enough to hear Jayden.

"What do you think it means by, seek the treasure?" He asked, his question directed at Addy who appeared to be thinking hard, her forehead scrunched in concentration.

"Why don't we just ask it and see what it says," Addy suggested.

It clicked finally, who they were talking about, and determined to beat them to the punch I spoke to Ash first.

"What treasure?" I asked him. I'd heard him mention it before, but parrots would say all sorts of things, so I didn't really think about it.

"Squawk! Seek the treasure! Squawk!"

"But what does that mean? Are we meant to be pirates, has someone buried treasure someplace?" I asked, getting frustrated.

Ash didn't respond and before I could ask again, a roar echoed through the jungle. It sounded like a T-Rex from movies and suddenly I wasn't thinking about treasure any longer.

Whatever had been keeping me from freaking out,

suddenly broke and by the looks on everyone else's faces, they were feeling it too. We were lost in a jungle filled with dinosaurs and no way to get out! What do we do what do we...it was going to be fine. A sudden wash of comfort coming over me as Ash nuzzled against my neck.

I was still worried about the dinosaurs, but I felt calmed enough to deal with it. Looking around, I saw everyone had similar looks of determination.

"So, what do we do?" I asked, thinking of the two options we seemed to have. "We can look for the treasure, whatever that is, or we can find someplace safe and wait to be rescued."

"We should wait," Sofia said, petting her snake's head. "My father will send someone to look for me."

She seemed to really believe that, so much so, that I smiled and got ready to remind her that we'd gotten here by some weird magic, and he'd likely not find us anytime soon. Addy spoke first, though.

"I know it's crazy but think about it, Sofia. Us getting here was like magic and without more magic, we probably won't get back. I think our best option is to find this treasure and hope that there is magic inside that can return us home."

Jayden surprised me by responding next. "It might be too soon to be calling it magic. After all, any sufficiently advanced technology will appear like magic. I think it makes sense that we are just so far behind whoever or whatever did this technologically, that it seems like magic. But I think I agree, however we got here, it is unlikely someone will rescue us. Have you guys seen the sky?"

I hadn't really noticed anything, but it had been visible back at our camp. The other two shook their heads that they had not either and Jayden continued.

"The stars don't match up," Jayden said, as if that explained everything.

"Are you saying we are on another planet?" Addy said, suddenly wide-eyed.

"That is my best theory right now," Jayden said, his nervous tone returning.

"That's cool!" I said, smiling. "I mean, we are like astronauts now or space explorers! I wonder if we'll meet any aliens?"

Jayden looked at his small fox, its tail curled around his neck. "I think we already have."

My eyes went a bit wide, and I looked at Ash, really looked at him. "You think these things are aliens? But I feel like I've been best buds with Ash forever, almost like he's always been with me."

"Me too," Sofia said, petting her snake, Cory.

"Same," Addy said.

"Which is why I am so sure they are aliens," Jayden explained. "They seem to be able to tap into our emotions and help us. Or have you all forgotten about the crazy loud roar already? We should be terrified and I'm only slightly nervous."

"Let's get back to camp," I suggested, and everyone nodded.

We'd gotten maybe half the way back when I noticed something dangling from a large tree.

"What's this?" I asked, it was a rope with knots tied into it, but it was so covered with green moss that at first it appeared to be a vine.

"Oh wow, look up there!" Addy said, pointing up.

I looked up and my jaw fell open. In the branches, halfway up the tall tree, were square rooms and flat walkways connecting them. Someone had made a treehouse!

"Let's go check it out!" I said, trying to climb the rope. It proved harder than I expected, but I managed it. After a solid few minutes of climbing, I'd reached the top, followed closely behind by Addy. It looked like Jayden and Sofia weren't going to give it a try, as they were still standing on the ground.

CHAPTER 14
IS THAT A CRYSTAL MOUNTAIN?

-Addy-

There was no way I'd let Zack take all the credit for finding whatever there was to find up here! I was just as good a climber as he was, so I took off after him, and after only a few tries, I began to gain on him up the tall tree toward the treehouse.

Cappy sat gently on my shoulder, okay with letting me do all the work. My arms began to burn just as we reached the top, and I took Zack's hand as he helped me into a square hole just big enough for us to squeeze through. No full-grown adult would be getting through that hole, that was for sure.

The room we found ourselves in was small and had two doors leading off to other larger rooms. We were high enough that a lot more light poured into the room than below, but I still used my skill to bring a globe of light. I wasn't about to let Zack out level me so easily.

Surprisingly, it seemed to be the right choice as the blank walls suddenly lit up as my light reflected off a shiny substance on the walls. Someone had written words all over the walls and in a language I recognized!

"This is Latin, I can read some of it," I said, elbowing Zack. He had been looking out toward one of the bigger rooms and hadn't noticed yet.

"Whoa, is that Spanish or something?" Zack asked, reaching out and touching the reflective words.

"I just said it was Latin, pay attention," I scolded him and leaned closer to begin translating.

Zack got bored after only a minute and left the room to explore. I wished I had Jayden's notebook suddenly and peeked down to see if they had changed their minds about coming up. But no, both of them stood down below like tiny little ants.

"Okay, focus Addy, you got this," I told myself getting back to reading the words.

Iter ad montem crystallum desinit cum saxum elementatum colligitur. Si redieris, domi eris.

Iter meant either path, journey, road, or travel. Okay so Iter ad montem meant 'path to the mountain' or more of a journey to the mountain, but the word cystallum meant...

"Journey to Crystal Mountain," I said, saying the words aloud to better remember them. I felt Cappy nuzzle against my neck, as if to say I was on the right track.

Okay I got this, what is next. Desinit cum saxum basically meant ending with a rock and then there was elementatum, I wasn't sure what that meant but by context I guessed it was saying, 'Journey to Crystal Mountain ends with an elemental rock.' What did that mean? Oh, I missed colligitur which means...to collect or is collected. So, it says, 'Journey to Crystal Mountain ends when the elemental rock is collected.'

"Zack, I figured out the first bit!" I called out, excited but still unsure what any of it meant. He didn't respond, so I went right back to my work.

Si redieris, domi eris.

'If you return or come back...' is the first part and domi mean at home or home something, so 'you will be at home.

"If you come back, you will be at home," I said, giving it my best guess. "Journey to Crystal Mountain ends when the elemental rock is collected. If you come back, you will be at home."

"Does that mean we can go home if we collect a rock?" Zack asked, startling me.

"I think we are onto something," I said, barely able to hold back my excitement. "If we collect this elemental rock and take it to whatever the Crystal Mountain is, then we might be able to get home!"

"Is that the Crystal Mountain," Zack asked, pointing out the doorway.

I moved over to where he stood and looked. We were high enough that in the distance I could see a massive mountain and it looked really odd. It reflected light and almost seemed to be on fire because of it, but as the sun shifted slightly, I saw the truth. Even from this distance, I could tell that the mountain looked like it was made of transparent crystal!

"Maybe this map will show us the way," Zack said, passing over a rolled-up piece of thick, smooth paper.

Unrolling it, I saw what looked like an old style map, with a compass at the bottom and the outline of a large island with a mountain in the middle labeled, 'Crystal Mountain' in Latin. We were on the right track. Nothing else was labeled but I could make out a detailed drawing of the cave we'd camped outside of and a few paths through the jungle, likely where we'd already been. Everywhere else had a very loose and fuzzy outline on it, as if us not being there was keeping the map from showing it to us properly.

"It's like it won't show us where we haven't been," I said, running my hand down the map. I felt a slight warmth come from it and I pulled my hand back. Paper maps were not meant to be warm. "I think it's a magical map." As soon as the words were out of my lips, the tree began to shake and creak.

"I don't know how stable this place is," Zack said, suddenly alert. "We should get out of here while we still can."

For once, I agreed with him, and shoved the map in my jeans' pocket. Zack waited for me, I slipped down the rope, twice as fast as I'd gone up it. Within a minute, I'd made it to the bottom and Zack was right behind me.

"We gotta move!" I yelled, as pieces of the treehouse began to break off above us. We ran as fast as we could toward our cave camp, but what we found there wasn't much better than what we were running from.

CHAPTER 15
RUN!

-Zack-

The campsite had been totally messed up! The bedrolls I spent so much effort on had been ripped into pieces, rocks had been thrown all around, and our campfire was nowhere to be seen.

"What in the heck happened?" I asked, turning to the group.

"I think something big walked through here," Jayden said, adjusting his glasses.

"What's that noise?" Sofia asked, but no one acknowledged her, we were all too busy inspecting the wrecked campsite.

"We might as well get cleaning," Addy said, walking toward the mouth of the cave.

I looked toward her and something in the back of my mind pushed through to the front. This was something I'd wondered several times but each time the thought would escape me until this very moment.

We'd not explored more than a dozen feet into the cave, and it kept going, getting bigger even, but never had anyone of us asked what may lie beyond in the shadows. I had a really bad feeling as Addy got closer. Running forward, I shouted at her.

"Wait, don't get too close!" But my words came too late, she'd already made it to the mouth of the cave. The noise Sofia had heard, I finally heard it too, sounded like breathing. Something huge was breathing from inside the cave!

Suddenly, a roar split the air and I was driven to my knees by how much it hurt my ears. I struggled to stand and looked to see Addy running toward us. She had a look of utter terror on her face, and when I looked behind her, I knew why.

The king of all dinosaurs, the mighty T-Rex, stepped out of the shadows and into the light. It filled the space of the massive cave opening and had overly large feet, little arms, and a mouth big enough to swallow a car. But that wasn't the most terrifying part about it, for some reason it had glowing red eyes and its dinosaur skin, both reptilian and feathered like a bird in a few places, had streaks of red mixed in as well.

"Squawk! RUN FOR IT! Squawk!"

Ash didn't need to tell me twice, I turned and helped Sofia then Jayden to their feet, making sure all three of my friends were in front of me before taking the rear. What could I do to slow this thing down? Nothing I had to craft would be useful, why hadn't I thought of a bigger trap! Now wasn't the time to think, now was the time to run.

So, we ran, the earth around us shook, the sound of trees falling filled our ears. I spared a glance behind me, I had to see what was happening. A tree smashed down right behind us, and I increased my sprint. Mr. Redeye the T-Rex, was slamming into smaller trees and knocking them down in its haste to follow us through the more densely filled jungle.

If we kept this up, we might actually outrun a T-Rex!

That is when I crested the top of a small hill and fell suddenly downward. I slid for several seconds before crashing into something below me. It turned out to be Jayden and he groaned in pain. I looked around, Addy had summoned light already, so it was easy to see. We'd somehow gotten ourselves trapped in a hole, maybe eight feet deep and barely wide enough for us all to stand close together.

My body pressed against Addy's and suddenly I was very aware of how nice she smelled, despite us being out in the jungle and running from dinosaurs. Focus! I told myself, trying not to picture what would happen when the T-Rex reached us.

"What do we do?" I asked, coming up with nothing myself.

"P-perhaps it won't see where we fell, and we'll be alright?" Jayden said, his teeth chattering in fear.

"Here it comes, quiet," Addy whispered.

Sofia was whimpering louder than she ought to if we didn't want to get caught, so I turned to her. We met eye to eye, and I could tell she was scared. I shifted over and wrapped my arms around her, thinking I'd try and comfort her. Her snake hissed at me, but Sofia actually pushed into my shoulder and began to cry.

All the while, the ground around us shook and another ear-splitting roar sounded from above.

"It found us!" Jayden screamed.

I looked up to see a glowing red eye looking down at us. With massive feet, it began to dig into our hole, taking a foot of dirt away with each stroke.

A sudden warmth ran through my body, and I felt calm. I could see that the others were feeling it too. Suddenly, I had plans. I grabbed hold of some roots, there were so many, then dirt, and stones. Putting my hand on as many as I could, I began to imagine what I'd be able to do with them.

I pictured a barrier of sharpened rocks and hard-packed dirt between us and the T-Rex, but no, if it broke, sharp rocks would come crashing down on us. After several long seconds, I came up with an ingenious idea. Instead of building with all the material, I imagined that I could craft a larger, deeper area beneath us.

It worked, a sudden whoosh of power and we fell several feet into a flat hardback dirt cube. I placed my hands on the side and widened it another space. We were now at least four feet deeper, but not out of the woods yet.

"I have an idea!" Addy cried out suddenly. And not too soon, because the T-Rex widened the hole several feet more than it had been, giving it a big enough space to reach down. "Gather close!"

We did so, all clutching at each other, but with determined looks on our faces. Addy held up her arm and light poured out like a fountain of water all around us. The transparent light took on a hazy look and suddenly we couldn't see the dinosaur as well anymore.

It reached down with its giant maw and closed around the large bowl of light that covered us.

Clank! Clank! Clank!

As hard as it might try, it wasn't able to break through. Whatever Addy had done, however she'd created the shield of light, it was enough to hold the T-Rex at bay. Because of the hole and how it had limited space to open its mouth, the T-Rex was limited in what else to try. It did use its massive feet to scratch at the shield, but my hardened ground and Addy's shield held firm.

Our companions all stayed close, their comfort rolling over us in waves. Even Sofia had stopped crying, instead we waited and waited some more. After what felt like forever, the T-Rex left, the jungle rumbling under its steps as it went to find an easier source of food.

"Way to go, Addy," I said, looking at her for the first time since the T-Rex left. Her face was covered in sweat and her forehead had turned a deep white color. A moment after I spoke, her eyes fluttered shut and I caught her as she passed out. The shield around us shattered into a hundred twinkling lights.

CHAPTER 16
CAMP 2.0

-Addy-

I came to, still in the hole we'd been trapped in for the last hour. Zack held me in his arms, with Jayden and Sofia close by. He looked so strong, looming over me with his bright blue eyes and look of concern.

"I've got you," he said, and I felt myself swoon a little. It only took a moment to snap out of my delusions, as memories flooded back into my head.

"Help me up," I said, going over what I'd done to get us out of that impossible situation.

It all came from the phrase 'hard light' that my Light Globe ability used. I reasoned that if I could harden light, then maybe I could make some kind of barrier. The only drawback was how the skill formed, without reading about it I had felt what was required. It was a channeled skill that require my focus and a charge per minute. If that T-Rex had stayed around for any longer, I'd have been done for. As it happened, I felt—again without even looking—that I'd leveled up to 3 and my charges were restored.

I checked just to be sure.

Light Weaver: Level 3, 2% Experience towards the next Level, 20/20 Charges Remaining.

New Skill Unlocked! Light Barrier: Projects a shell of light over an area from your Soul Band. (Warning! This skill takes 1 charge to activate and 1 per minute to maintain, as well as bearer must maintain focus the entire time.)

"We should get moving," I said, patting Cappy on the head. Somehow I knew he had something to do with me discovering how to use a new skill on my Soul Band.

"We need to figure out what our copper bands do," Jayden said, looking to Sofia. "We might have the means to protect ourselves and not even know it."

"I just want to get out of this nightmare, not fight back," Sofia said, frowning.

I saw Zack look over to her and they met eyes for a second, before Sofia blushed and looked away. Was there something going on between them, I wondered. I'd seen how Zack had held her tight when she was panicking, but that didn't mean anything, did it?

Pushing away my silly thoughts, I followed Zack's lead, scrambling up the side of the hill that the T-Rex had flattened while trying to eat us.

What we needed now was a better place to hide, if that treehouse hadn't fallen apart it would have been the perfect place. That is when I got an awesome idea.

"We should build a treehouse!" I said, then looking to Zack I asked, "Do you think you could do that, with your crafting?"

"I think so," Zack said, walking fast in a new direction, this time away from the cave where we'd spent time the night before. "I don't know how I'll get the supplies high enough to make floors though."

"We can set up a rudimentary pully system if you can make sturdy rope and get high enough," Jayden said, stepping up beside Zack.

"Does it have to be a treehouse?" Sofia asked, we all looked at her, surprised she'd decided to weigh in on the conversation.

I suddenly remembered something about Sofia that I'd learned the summer before when we'd gone to a theme park together. She was afraid of heights.

"What, are you afraid of heights or something?" Zack asked, laughing. He didn't look back, because if he did, he'd seen the red-faced look of shame that Sofia suddenly had.

"It's alright to be scared of heights," I said, putting my

arm around her and shooting an angry look at Zack when he turned to look at Sofia. He seemed to get it, and made a face that said, 'Oops I'm an idiot' or at least that is how I imagined it.

Zack opened his mouth again and nonsense spilled forth. "It's not like we need your help, I will make it plenty safe and then you just have to get up there."

"Shut up already," I said. Zack seemed confused at my censure, but I just shook my head. Boys are so dumb sometimes.

We kept walking until we started to hear a sound that made Sofia perk up.

"We are close to a beach!" She announced, surprising us all by rushing forward into the dense brush. She ran wide around Zack, who had fashioned another ancient looking machete to cut plants from our path. I really didn't like the idea of giving him a weapon, but I kept my words to myself for now. He'd nearly cut his hand off on several occasions.

"Sofia, wait!" I called out, following Jayden as we took a wide path around Zack and followed after Sofia.

Sure enough, just through the dense brush, we stumbled out onto a beach, but not like one I'd ever seen before. The sand looked like salt and pepper. Black and white mixed so finely that it looked like seasoning spread over the entire length of the beach. The water, luckily, seemed normal enough and I joined Sofia, who had already pulled her shoes off and had her feet in the off-looking sand.

"It's so warm, I love it!" She exclaimed. I reached down, not yet willing to put my bare feet in such an odd looking beach, and scooped up a handful.

Smelling it, I decided it smelled like I expected; a bit of a salty, earthy smell. When Sofia didn't cry out or complain of anything, I took a page from her book, and slipped my shoes off. I buried my feet into the sand up to my ankles and enjoyed the soothing, warming that came with it.

"There is a pretty sturdy tree just a ways down from here," Zack announced. "Let's collect plants so I can craft rope and then maybe get some wood too."

I nodded along, lost in the comforting warmth of the beach. Jayden and Zack left us alone while they began working. After about five minutes, I sighed and got up to help as well.

"Let's go Sofia, we should help collect supplies and maybe some berries, I'm hungry," I said, brushing sand from my feet to slip my shoes back on.

"I'm good," Sofia said, laying back into the warm sand.

"Seriously, let's help," I said, getting a little annoyed.

"I'm. Good." She annunciated each word and closed her eyes. She snake-crawled to her stomach and curled up there.

"Whatever," I said, feeling annoyed, but not wanting to start a fight over it.

It took over an hour, but we got enough plant material together for him to make a massively long rope. All that was left was climbing the tree. Luckily it had low branches, ones Zack suggested we cut off after making the treehouse, and soon he was a dozen feet higher than the T-Rex had been, which was to say, plenty safe.

Picking out the thickest of branches, he slung the rope over and Jayden caught it, tying bundles of wood that had already been converted to wooden planks by Zack, while I rested. Lifting the wood up, which took all that Jayden and I had strength wise, Zack turned in into our first platform.

It was amazing how his skills molded with the environment surrounding it. There were supports, and the wood was cut perfectly around the branches to stabilize it. Zack had to come down, because we needed more wood, like A LOT of it. If we had a faster way of collecting and bringing wood up, things would go faster, but as it stood, we'd need to find food soon or we'd be too hungry.

"I'm hungry," Sofia said, making me jump. I hadn't seen her approach.

"Maybe if you'd help we'd already have berries collected," I shot back. The strenuous lifting had given me an ache in my back and made me cranky.

Sofia looked hurt but didn't say anything in response.

"Let's go find berries," I said, grabbing her hand so she couldn't say no. She let herself be led off and together we searched for berries.

"I'm sorry," Sofia said, as we began to pick some of the sweet ones we'd eaten raw before. "I'm not used to camping and doing stuff. I wish my daddy would come find me already."

I tried not to be, but I was still really annoyed. "Your dad isn't coming, Sofia. Neither is mine. We are here and we have to rely on each other. Every one of us needs to pull their weight until we get back."

"I know," Sofia said, tears forming at the edge of her eyes. Her snake coiled close and hissed at me. Sofia blinked, a look of determination on her face. "I'll do better! Watch, I'll bring back so much wood that they'll be happy."

She filled her arms with branches and as she tried to grab another, suddenly they disappeared. Sofia stumbled forward, confused.

"Are you okay, what happened?" I asked, looking around her trying to see where the branches had dropped.

She smiled suddenly and touched her bracelet.

Space: Level 1, 10% Experience towards the next Level, 9/10 Charges Remaining.

New Skill Unlocked! Inventory: Using your Soul Band you can store things inside interdimensional space for the cost of 1 charge per transfer. Manifesting Items back does not cost any Charges.

"Holy cow!" I said, mimicking something my dad liked to say.

"I figured out my stupid ugly bracelet!" Sofia said, jumping up and down in joy. "I'm useful!"

Testing the bounds of her new skill, we gathered a very large pile of wood, rocks, and leaves. With a single charge she scooped them all up, just by placing her hands on them.

The treehouse came together much faster after that. We still had to haul the items up because Sofia refused to try and climb, but with the large amounts she brought and a special pully that Jayden helped Zack create, we had a working, small treehouse by nightfall.

Zack even made a step ladder and with all of our encouragement, we managed to get Sofia to climb up it.

We were doing it one day at a time. Now if only we weren't so darn thirsty.

CHAPTER 17
DODO BIRDS!

-Zack-

Our second night in the jungle was better than the first. I discovered that with wood and moss I could make literal beds, so I did so while everyone else collected berries and searched for water. Sofia's new skills came in handy; we had large stores of food, wood, and even fresh water stored in little water containers made from leaves. It became a craftable item, but they barely worked, leaking more than it should.

I was walking the beach with Jayden, going into the jungle to check my many spiked hole traps I'd made, but so far no luck.

"What is that?" Jayden asked, pointing down the beach.

I looked and had to squint to make it out. It was like a fat chicken with an oversized beak. Just as I was about to answer that it looked like a funky chicken, Jayden spoke up again.

"That's a dodo bird!"

"That's a weird name," I said, as it waddled right toward us but didn't look threatening at all. I had my machete, and an idea crossed my mind.

"They went extinct hundreds of years ago and were said to be extremely docile," Jayden said, adjusting his glasses.

I raised my machete and decided I would do what I needed to so that we could eat meat. "I'm going to make this one extinct and cook up some tasty meat," I said, walking up to the bird.

Jayden adverted his eyes while I went to work getting the bird ready. It didn't take long and soon I was up to my elbows in gore and feathers. I left the guts and feathers on the beach, taking the meat back to our treehouse.

I'd set up a fireplace built into a section of the tree-house separate from the rest, just in case fire became an issue. Soon, meat covered in berry juice was cooked into tasty morsels. The recipe was called sweet berry stew and through the magic of crafting, it had flavors like salt and pepper, despite the fact I hadn't added any.

"I can't believe you killed a bird," Sofia said, refusing the meat I offered.

Addy gave me a look as well, but she gobbled down the meat without question. Sure, they could be mad at me, but we needed to eat, and this was the way.

We had leftover meat, but Sofia refused to store it away, meaning it would likely go to waste.

The air around us was warm as the sun rose high into the sky and a sudden noise, like an intense chirping, sounded from below. I looked over the edge and what I saw, made me stand in surprise.

A freaking raptor with orange and blue stripes and colorful feathers running down its back stood not far from the bottom of our treehouse hideout. I could just make out its snout covered in blood, and instantly knew I had made a mistake when I left out the dodo bird remains.

"Jayden," I said, looking where the rope ladder hung. "Can raptors climb rope ladders?"

"What? No, I don't think so," Jayden said, looking over the edge to where I watched the raptor. "Holy crap, it's a Utah Raptor!"

"A Utah Raptor?" Addy asked, nudging me to the side to get a look.

"It's fine, we are safe this far up, aren't we?" Sofia chimed in staying far from the edge and not looking.

The raptor jumped onto a branch, one of the higher ones that I'd not thought to cut down. Crap.

Jayden began to whimper, looking around until he saw the meat lying on some linen. I watched him as he grabbed it up and tossed some over the edge. "Maybe if we feed it, it'll go away," Jayden said, throwing another piece.

I left him to do it and kept back what I wanted to say. I thought it was more likely that if we fed it, then it'd come back and maybe bring friends, but I waited and watched to see what would happen.

The first chunk of meat hit the raptor in the head and it shook it off a moment later, actually catching it as it flung into the air. It reminded me of a dog performing a trick where it flipped a treat off its nose and caught it in one single motion. The next piece fell right into its mouth, and then it jumped even higher, perching on a thick branch only a dozen feet away.

That is when something weird happened. I looked over to Jayden and he seemed to be glowing. Then when I looked back at the raptor, I saw it was too. Mechanically, Jayden threw the last chunk of meat and suddenly the glow disappeared.

"I f-figured out what Bondsmith means," Jayden said, never taking his eyes off the raptor. "Meet Charles the raptor, I've tamed him. I can tame dinosaurs!"

Bondsmith: Level 2, 5% Experience towards the next Level, 10/15 (5 being held to hold Raptor Bond) Charges Remaining.

New Skill Unlocked! Tame Beasts Rank 1: Project your bonds of friendship onto a target for 12 hours, causing them to follow orders and become protective. Rank 1 means they will follow simple orders; higher ranks will increase bonded creature's intelligence.

CHAPTER 18
BIG TROUBLE
RETURN TO BOOK 2 FOR THE NEXT EXCITING INSTALLMENT

-Addy-

"Are we sure this is a good idea?" I asked for the third time as Zack constructed a special shelter for the raptor on the ground.

Jayden had 'tamed' it and since then, it acted more like a loyal dog than the fierce predator that it clearly was. I stood the farthest away, even Sofia seemed to be warming up to it. Something about the look in its eyes made me wary, like any moment it might revert back to its former state.

"It'll be fine, as long as I feed it meat before the twelve hours is up," Jayden explained, seeing me take another step away. "Charles likes you, come pet him."

Jayden seemed so much less nervous than he'd been this entire time, like having a dinosaur under his command gave him an extra bout of confidence.

"I'm okay right here," I said, wondering how effective my light attack would be on the raptor if things went sideways.

"Do you think you'll be able to tame that T-Rex if it comes back for us?" Zack asked. He was literally petting the raptor at this point.

"I doubt it," Jayden said. "From what little I am understanding about my taming skill, I was lucky to have gotten a raptor on my first try. Anything bigger and I'd need way too much meat and a higher level."

"I've got some ideas for traps, ones I could set up around the treehouse or that could be dropped from above, Sofia you want to help me?" Zack asked, Sofia shot him a look, but nodded her assent.

I decided I would go practice my Beam of Light skill while they worked on their stuff. Plus, any reason to get away from the scary dinosaur was a good enough reason for me.

Focusing, I felt a charge whoosh away from me as a beam of light shot into a nearby tree. I stood far enough away that only Cappy could hear me, so I decided it would be alright to monologue.

"This has all been really cool, sort of," I said, Cappy nudged my neck and I felt a soothing warmth pass over me. "But how does any of this help us get home? We just need to find the elemental stone and go to the crystal mountain, whatever that means."

I played over in my head what I would do when I got back, hug my parents, tell them how much I missed them, and then call the cops on Mr. Shadow.

The ground shook suddenly and from a considerable distance I heard the roar of a T-Rex. It was a sound I'd never forget for as long as I lived. Pictures and even movies didn't do justice to the bone chilling terror that it invoked.

I made my way back to the ground a few minutes later and saw an odd sight. Four dodo birds now followed Jayden around like lost puppies. Jayden and Zack were having an argument.

"It doesn't feel right to let you kill one that I've tamed," Jayden was saying.

While Zack came back with, "Then why'd you tame all the ones we found? You said yourself that you need meat to keep the bond strong with Charles, so which dodo is lunch?"

"But I've named them already, Galileo, Edison, Hawking, and Archimedes don't deserve to die," Jayden said, pointing at each as he named them.

"Pick one," Zack warned, lifting his machete. That was when Charles the raptor stepped between him and the dodo birds, letting off a dangerous growl.

Zack dropped the machete, and his eyes went wide.

"It's okay Charles, calm down," Jayden said, petting the feathers that ran along the raptor's spine.

Charles calmed down and nuzzled the fox around Jayden's neck.

Zack started walking back down the beach, calling over his shoulder, "I'm going to find a wild dodo for lunch, be back soon."

Hadn't he heard the T-Rex roar? It might be close enough to be a problem. I decided I couldn't leave him alone, so I told Jayden that it would be best to get up high and then I ran after Zack.

"Come to join the hunt?" Zack asked, laughing as I stumbled over a rock in the sand.

"We should hurry, I think the T-Rex is close," I said, watching the edge of the jungle for any movement.

"It'll be fine," Zack said, brushing me off. Despite what he said I noticed he increased his walking speed significantly. None of us wanted to encounter that T-Rex again.

We found a dodo bird and Zack did his thing, using a knife to disembowel it. It was messy work and I stayed back, not wanting to get blood all over myself. After he finished, I held the dodo bird by its feet while Zack cleaned off in the ocean water.

Despite being on the beach the night before, there didn't seem to be much of a tide, the water staying basically where it was during the day. It made me wonder if the presence of two moons, I'd noticed last night, made a difference to the ocean currents.

A roar, much closer this time, cut through the jungle. A pack of wild dodo charged onto the sand a little farther down the beach, and to my utter astonishment, the T-Rex with glowing red eyes followed them, scooping up one in its mouth.

"RUN!" I screamed, Zack turned and met my eyes. Together we sprinted as fast as we could toward the tree-house. The T-Rex didn't seem to notice us until we were basically back, another roar splitting the air as it began to shake the ground on its way toward us.

No, no, no, no!

Zack took the dodo and began to climb up below me. The raptor and Jayden's dodos looked around wildly but did nothing.

We reached the top just as the T-Rex lumbered up to the tree. If it were any bigger it would be able to scoop us up in its mouth I realized.

"Jayden, have your pets attack!" Zack yelled as he threw the dead dodo aside and made it to the top of the rope ladder.

"Alright," Jayden said, and I looked over the edge to see.

His team of five dodos and raptor had moved away

from the treehouse and were currently being ignored by the T-Rex, its red eyes locked up at us.

"We need to deal with this thing once and for all," I said, aiming my arm and ready to give it all I had.

"Right!" Zack said. "Sofia, start throwing the rocks you gathered down on it, and I will trigger the traps we set up. Jayden, focus on guiding your raptor, and Addy, hit it with light!"

A part of me pushed back from Zack taking control, but I went with it, as I'd already planned to do as much. I'd used two charges and had 23 more since reaching level 4. Looking down at the monstrous T-Rex I took aim and fired.

My attack zapped it right in the nose and left a trail of smoke curling up into the air, but otherwise did nothing. This was going to be harder than we thought.

Zack pulled loose a rope and rocks tumbled down hitting the T-Rex and causing it to shake its head in annoyance. Suddenly, an even bigger pile of rocks appeared just above its head, smashing down and staggering it back. Sofia looked over the edge, her face green from how high up she was. She fell backward, having done all she could by emptying her inventory.

Jayden yelled suddenly, "Get 'em!"

I looked over after firing another shot and saw Jayden's five dodos and hisraptor charging forward. The T-Rex wasn't going to notice them, and I would keep it that way. I aimed for the eyes and shot again, this time it caused the T-Rex to roar, and hurt my ears.

I looked down again just in time to see three dodos smashed into red slush by the T-Rex, but two made it through and smashed their heads against the enormous predator's feet, doing nothing.

Luckily, Charles the raptor was another thing altogether. He jumped at the last minute, taking a bloody bite into the T-Rex's neck and swinging itself over the top.

Working as best I could without hitting Charles, I shot light-infused shot after shot, until I had 6 charges left and an idea hit me.

If I could make hard light, perhaps I can make a spear of hard light or something more likely to do some damage. I focused on my intent, sending a mental image of what I imagined until it felt like it was working. Then, I reared back my arm as if throwing a javelin and thrust it forward. The familiar whooshing followed and a ten-foot-long spear of light launched forward at the T-Rex.

Somewhere in my head I felt that that had taken 2 charges and I only had 4 more to go! Zack was collapsing other parts of the treehouse, hoping the wood would do something, but it didn't.

The raptor had been caught in the T-Rex's mouth and thrown off. Charles the raptor faced off against the T-Rex, and then started making an odd chirping sound.

As the T-Rex rose up, a javelin of light smashed into

its wounded back, causing it to whip its head back in our direction. Two more charges.

Charles took the momentary advantage and bit hard on the T-Rex's leg. Wrong move, I thought, as the T-Rex kicked outward and sent Charles flying into the jungle.

I heard the chirping calling noise again, and suddenly there were several more chirping sounds than just the one. I raised my hand, ready to throw my last javelin when from out of the thick brush four raptors appeared. Charles, bloody and injured, led a pack of three raptors right for the T-Rex!

They worked together as a team, biting, cutting, and dodging. The T-Rex was finally getting what it deserved!

"Way to go Charles!" I yelled as Jayden cheered behind me.

But just when it began to look like we'd win, Charles ducked when he should have dodged. The T-Rex clamped its massive jaws down on the raptor, lifting it into the air.

"No you won't!" I screamed, raising my arm in the air I took aim for the red eyes and let loose my last javelin. It soared through the air while Charles thrashed to get free. With a satisfying smash, it drove deep into the T-Rex's eye.

The other eye suddenly stopped being red and instead a confused looking T-Rex shook its head, releasing Charles in the process. The T-Rex roared, but it was nothing like the roars that had come before, this one almost sounded upset. Then it charged past the remaining raptors, running off into the jungle.

Charles laid hurt on the ground, but the other raptors chased after the T-Rex, not ready to give up the hunt.

For now, I knew that our worries with the T-Rex were over. Something about the angry red that had glowed from its eyes and the red fading away, made me think the poor T-Rex wasn't completely in control of what it was doing.

There was something larger at work, I just didn't know what.

"We need to find the Elemental Stone and take it to Crystal Mountain," I said, turning to face my friends. "Are you with me?"

They all nodded their heads and suddenly Ash the parrot spoke.

"Squawk! Check the map! Squawk!"

Zack pulled free the map and turned it over to show us. New areas had been revealed on the map as well as markers that read, "Elemental Stone" in Latin, along with a dotted path we could take to find it.

"All this time?" I asked, looking at the map. "The Elemental Stone is in the cave we camped out in on the first night, but it looks like it goes much deeper. We have our work cut out for us, but we will prevail!"

Jayden stood proudly, his nerves at ease for now. Sofia, still nervous from the heights, stood as well, ready for anything. Zack had begun checking the treehouse for damage, but I knew he'd given it his all.

Together there was nothing we wouldn't be able to accomplish.

LEAVE A REVIEW

Thank you for reading. Please leave a review.

Check out my website at AuthorTimothyMcGowen.com

If you really liked the book, please consider reaching out and telling me what you enjoyed about it at, Timothy. mcgowen1@gmail.com.

Join my Facebook group and discuss the books at: https://www.facebook.com/groups/234653175151521/

Join my Patreon at: https://www.patreon.com/TimothyMcGowen

ABOUT THE AUTHOR

Timothy McGowen was born in Modesto, California. His journey into stories started with reading the Goosebumps books. Later he read a novel by Terry Brooks and became hooked on fantasy/scifi almost instantly. Shortly after that he was given a school assignment to write a 5 page fiction story, and 25 pages later his story was half done. He hasn't stopped writing since.

His popular Arcane Knight series has sold thousands of copies in both ebook and audible so far. Consider signing up for my newsletter for news on book releases as they become available.

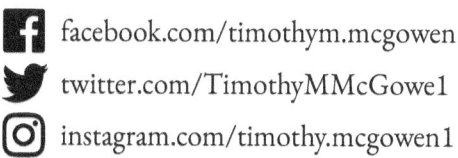

facebook.com/timothym.mcgowen

twitter.com/TimothyMMcGowe1

instagram.com/timothy.mcgowen1

LITRPG GROUP

Check out this group if you want to gather together and hear about new great LitRPG books.

(https://www.facebook.com/groups/LitRPGGroup/)

LEARN MORE ABOUT LITRPG/GAMELIT GENRE

To learn more about LitRPG & GameLit, talk to author and just have an awesome time by joining some LitRPG/Gamelit groups.

Here is another LitRPG group you can join if you are looking for the next great read!

Faccbook.com/groups/LitRPG.books

List of LitRPG/Gamelit Facebook Groups:

- https://www.facebook.com/groups/LitRPGReleases/
- https://www.facebook.com/groups/litrpgforum/
- https://www.facebook.com/groups/litrpglegends/
- https://www.facebook.com/groups/LitRPGsociety/

- https://www.facebook.com/groups/AleronKong/